COUNTDOWN TO CHRISTMAS

Adam & Charlotte Guillain

Pippa Curnick

EGMONT

"We're counting down to **Christmas!**"
Cheered a very jolly bear.
He called a meeting in the woods
And *everyone* was there!

"Come, gather round," called Bear. "Be quick!"
His voice boomed deep and loud.

Mouse grabbed her scarf and mittens
and she ran to join the crowd.

"I've made a **Christmas game**," said Bear.
"It ends with a **surprise**.
I'll call a name out every day
To go and find a **prize**."

"Me first!" begged Mouse. "Oh, *please* choose me!"
"No, me!" cried everyone.
But Bear smiled at young Hedgehog and
He said, "You're **NUMBER 1!**"

When Hedgehog found her special prize,
She rolled head-over-heels.
"Oh, look! **A toy!**" she squeaked with joy.
"A lovely **cow on wheels!**"

But next day Toad got **NUMBER 2** -
And found a **pair of ears**.

Mouse laughed. "You're like a **donkey** now!"
Toad huffed and muttered, "Cheers!"

Raccoon had **NUMBER 3** and cried,
"I've got a **candy cane!**"

When Frog and Chipmunk found the same
They cheered, "Yay! **Sweets** again!"

But Badger grumbled, **"Huh!** What's *this*?"
Confusion in his eyes.

Mouse smiled and squeaked, "A **tea towel!** Ooh!
That's quite a **useful** prize."

Then Squirrel found a pair of **wings**

And Weasel got the same.

"Now I've got wings as well!" sneered Rat.
"**Bah!** What a *silly* game!"

Some creatures started moaning then:
"These prizes aren't *that* great."

"But Bear has a **surprise** for us!"
Squeaked Mouse. "We need to wait!"

The next day there were **paper chains**,

Then **baubles** . . .

and
some
lights.

12

Mouse jumped with joy:

"They'll brighten up
These long dark winter nights!"

But then the **thirteenth** day arrived,
And Beaver got . . . some **straw!**
"That's not a prize!" she sniffed, and then

She **threw it on the floor!**

13

Mouse called, "There'll be a reason! Please!
We **must** believe in Bear!"

But Beaver simply
stomped away
And mumbled,
"It's not fair."

Then in the morning Mouse woke up
And coughed and sneezed –

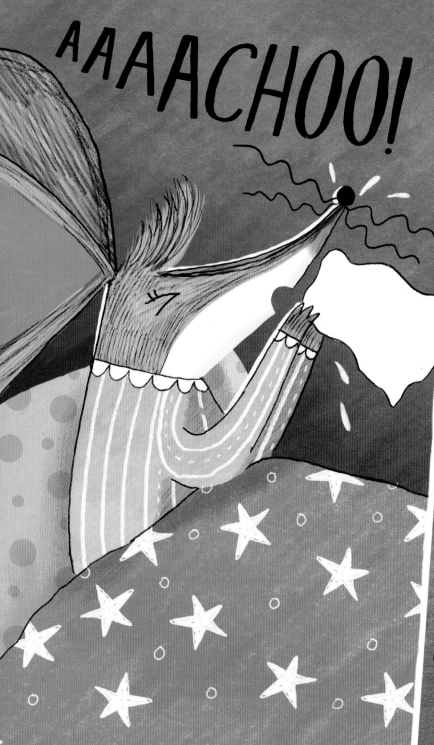

AAAACHOO!

"**Oh, no!** I'll have to stay in bed.
I think I've caught the flu."

She didn't see Mole find a crown,

Nor Skunk,

nor Porcupine.

15

16

The animals agreed **these** gifts
Were really rather fine!

For two more days, Mouse felt quite ill.
She huddled in her shawl.
"But what if Bear forgets **my** turn?
He might – I'm rather **small**."

But, while she fretted, Bunny found
A **basket**, like a bed.

Then Mrs Bear cried, "Ooh! **A scarf!**"
And wrapped it round her head.

At last Mouse poked her nose outside.
"Perhaps it's my turn now?"

But **NUMBER 19** went to **Owl** –

"I've got some lanterns – wow!"

The next day, Bear chose Deer, who found

A holly wreath – "Hurray!"

Then fox cubs – one, two, three – found **hats**

And scampered off to play.

When finally the last day came,
Mouse hoped with all her might:
"It *surely* must be my turn now.
There's only **one more night!**"

Mouse sat and waited **all day long**
As footsteps passed her house.

She sobbed,
"They've **all** forgotten me!"
But then a voice called . . .

"Mouse!"

She crept out of her burrow where
The moon was glowing bright.
A beaming Bear said merrily,

"It's Christmas Eve tonight!"

He handed Mouse a wrapped-up box.
"Just open *this* and see."
Then Mouse pulled out . . .

. . . a shiny star!

Bear smiled, "Now come with me!"

He led Mouse through the frosty trees,
A twinkle in his eyes.

"Your friends have *not* forgotten you,"
He said. "Here's my . . .

. . . SURPRISE!

We've made our own **nativity**, with gifts for **everyone**.

"Your shining star's the final touch
— it's time for **Christmas fun!**"

For Charlotte's mum, Chris – thank you for
always making Christmas special. xx – CG & AG

To Finley and Ruby – wishing you the
merriest of Christmases, always – PC

EGMONT
We bring stories to life

First published in Great Britain 2019 by Egmont UK Limited
The Yellow Building, 1 Nicholas Road, London W11 4AN

www.egmont.co.uk

Text copyright © Adam & Charlotte Guillain 2019
Illustrations copyright © Pippa Curnick 2019

The moral rights of the authors and illustrator have been asserted.

ISBN 978 1 4052 8845 3